SCARY STORIES

FOR

A FRIGHT
IN THE NIGHT

SCARY STORIES

FOR

A FRIGHT
IN THE NIGHT

S.L. CLAYTOR

Darter Lane Books

Darter Lane
Books

ISBN-13: 978-1-950900-02-2
ISBN-10: 1-950900-02-9

CONTENTS

Vanderstein Castle. A stormy October night.

A door creaks open, and a pale man draped in a black cape greets five rain-drenched visitors.

"Good evening. Welcome to Vanderstein Castle."

The pale man listens as the visitors explain their plight of being stranded due to car trouble and having a two-hour wait for tow truck assistance.

"I'm glad you spotted Vanderstein Castle. I just inherited this old dwelling from my late uncle, and I am delighted to receive company. Please, come inside."

A bony hand gestures.

"Before moving here, I seldom entertained guests, and in the spirit of being a good host, I welcome you to wait here until the tow truck arrives."

A flash of lightning streaks across the sky as the door creaks shut with a hollow thud.

"I'm afraid the storm is disrupting electrical power, causing the lights to intermittently flicker on and off, but fear not, for this lantern will light our way. If you'll follow me down this dim corridor to the library, I believe I can procure a log for the fire, and while you warm yourselves, we can pass the time by reading some scary stories. I have one particular short story collection in mind that's sure to give you a fright in the night."

The host chuckles under his breath.

"Pay no mind to the portraits hanging on the walls. Their eyes are not actually following you. And those rattling chains, ghostly moans, and creaking hinges emanating from the dark reaches of the corridor, well...it is a very old castle."

The host glances back with a deadpan expression.

"Rest assured, there is nothing to fear, not even those distant, echoing footsteps. I'm sure they are merely reverberations of our own footfall."

The host stops at a tall wooden door.

"We have arrived at the library."

He pushes the door open, and a hairy spider drops from an overhanging cobweb.

"You'll find the room a bit dusty, but please, have a seat and get comfortable."

The host pulls an old log from a cobweb-covered stack of wood sitting next to a wide fireplace and places it on the inner hearth. After achieving a steady flame, he walks to a bookcase that stretches from floor to ceiling and pulls out a leather-bound book engraved with curious symbols.

"Yes, here it is: *Scary Stories for a Fright in the Night*. Now, if you're ready, this first story is called 'The Collectors.' It is one of my favorites."

THE COLLECTORS

L ate one night, a young man named Daniel and his girlfriend, Dawn, were driving home from a date, discussing the events of the night as they traveled a desolate country road that twisted and turned through the outskirts of a small town. Rounding a wide curve, the moonlit landscape cast an ominous aura that filled Daniel with a dreadful sense of unease.

"Lookout!" Dawn suddenly yelled when a large, dark object darted across the road in front of them.

Daniel slammed on the brakes of his truck, and the vehicle skidded onto the shoulder of the road, stopping a few feet shy of a small bridge that spanned a narrow creek.

"What the heck was that?" Dawn lowered her feet from the dash, having instinctively braced herself when Daniel hit the brakes.

Daniel pointed at what appeared to be a horse-drawn carriage that had ceased motion just past the bridge, near the entrance of Cemetery Road.

"Is that a horse and carriage?" Dawn's voice trembled. "Where on earth did it come from? Both sides of the road are fenced."

"I don't know." Daniel stared in bewilderment at the blotted form of a driver, searching for some distinguishable feature, but finding none. He had no explanation.

The carriage, enveloped by an eerie mist, then resumed motion and turned onto Cemetery Road. The sound of the horse's hooves striking the pavement echoed as the carriage quickly transitioned into little more than shadows, but a doleful melody drifted in its wake, haunting words sung in a faint but clear voice:

> *We are the collectors*
> *Collecting what is due*
> *We are the collectors*
> *Our harvest must ensue*

The harvest moon has risen
A harbinger of fate
The fullest moon of many
We wait to storm the gate

"I don't like this." Dawn's eyes widened with fright.

Daniel was baffled by the eerie encounter. "I couldn't see his eyes, but I know he was looking right at me, like he knew me. And that song...."

"Let's get out of here, Daniel. This is too creepy."

"I want to see where he goes." Daniel was overcome by a compelling need to follow the specter.

"Down Cemetery Road? Not a chance," Dawn adamantly refused. "We wouldn't have time anyway. It's nearly 11:00—my curfew," she reminded him. "Still, even if we had time, I wouldn't go. There's nothing at the end of that road but graves. You could not pay me enough to follow 'whatever that was' into the cemetery at night. Especially not tonight. Have you forgotten about the total lunar eclipse? It's happening right now. Look, the moon is already partially eclipsed."

At that moment, headlights from an approaching vehicle appeared behind them, and Daniel watched in the rearview mirror as a red car rolled to a stop alongside his truck. "Cathy." He immediately recognized Dawn's sister and lowered his window so the girls could talk.

"What's wrong?" Cathy asked. "Did your truck break down?"

"No, the truck's fine," Daniel assured her.

"Cathy, I am so glad to see you," Dawn told her sister. "You'll never believe what we just saw. It was the strangest thing."

"You can tell me about it when we get to the house. We only have a few minutes till curfew, so you better hurry home." Cathy started to raise her window.

"Wait." Daniel stopped her. "Dawn needs a ride."

"What?" Dawn's brow furrowed. "I can't believe this."

"I want to do a little investigating. I really want to see where that carriage went."

"I think you're crazy to follow whoever, or whatever, that was to the cemetery at night, but I won't attempt to stop you." Dawn got out of the truck. "Just be careful."

"Don't worry." Daniel flashed a smile. "I'll call you in a little while, when I get home."

The moment Dawn and Cathy drove away, Daniel pulled his truck onto the pavement, crossed the bridge, and made a right turn onto Cemetery Road. The entrance of the narrow lane, divided by two old oak trees, offered scarcely enough width for a vehicle to pass on either side of the sprawling trees. Laden with shadows, once beyond the entrance, the split lane merged into a single-lane roadway bordered by barbed wire fence that enclosed a multi-hundred-acre orange grove.

"Where are you?" Daniel lowered his window, searching for any sign of the mysterious horse and carriage, soon catching the faint, hypnotic sound of the specter's haunting tune as he neared the cemetery gate.

Rolling to a stop, he shut off the truck, got out, and glanced over the place of the dead that lay blanketed in a coppery, unearthly florescence. He glanced upward and saw that the eclipse was nearing totality as he eased toward the entrance and daringly entered the cemetery's sacred confines.

He stepped past a looming, white stone cross that stood the height of a giant just inside the gate and continued along a dirt path that separated the cemetery into two halves of rowed sections. Lured forth by the haunting tune that grew louder and clearer with each step he took, Daniel knew he would never forget the song's dark and foreboding lyrics:

> *We are the collectors*
> *Collecting what is due*
> *We are the collectors*
> *Our harvest must ensue*

The mighty orb is bleeding
We enter now to reap
The blessed blood is calling
And what we take, we keep

Daniel moved deeper and deeper into the cemetery that grew colder and colder with each step he took. He cautiously veered from the path and maneuvered around several headstones, stopping dead in his tracks when he came upon the silhouetted horse and carriage eerily resting amid a bed of low-lying mist.

Quickly ducking out of sight, Daniel took cover behind a large tree to escape detection. Crouched low, his breaths came quick, and his heart pounded with such intensity that he feared the specter might hear its desperate drum. Although well-concealed in the shadows, he couldn't shake an unnerving suspicion that the specter knew he was there. That the specter was, in fact, waiting for him.

"The mighty orb is bleeding," Daniel spoke in a hushed whisper, repeating the unsettling lyrics, wondering if the verse referred to the blood moon lunar eclipse that was currently occurring.

He glanced upward once again, remembering that this total lunar eclipse was not only a blood moon, but a harvest moon and a supermoon as well, which was a rare occurrence.

"We are the Collectors, collecting what is due." Daniel repeated another line from the specter's song, knowing he had heard those precise words before.

With that thought, a buried memory emerged of Daniel's father, who upon his deathbed had told him: "Beware the night of the super blood moon eclipse, for on such a night, harvesters cross worlds and take souls. These harvesters are known as the collectors, coming to collect what is due."

Daniel's father went on to tell of a selfish ancestor who had signed a contract with the harvesters, exchanging a thousand years of blood souls for personal power and wealth, a ruthless act of greed that cursed his bloodline, and to remain so until reaching the time of fulfillment. For only then would the debt be paid in full.

"A thousand years of blood souls." Daniel shuddered inside.

Being only ten at the time of his father's death, he hadn't taken the warning seriously, but now he feared the worst. The absolute worst.

Keeping a close eye on his subject, Daniel drew in a sharp gasp when the specter unexpectedly shifted his position and appeared to stare directly at him. Daniel dared not move, searching the dark void of the specter's featureless face, imagining a fearsome monster beneath the draped hood that concealed him. Not sure what to expect, Daniel fell into a maddening state of panic when the specter began to sing a third spine-chilling verse of his grim, foreboding song.

"No. I don't want to hear anymore." Daniel covered his ears, but there was no escaping the disquieting melody that drifted through the frigid air as if it had a life of its own:

> *We are the collectors*
> *Collecting what is due*
> *We are the collectors*
> *Our harvest must ensue*
>
> *We travel in the darkness*
> *Beneath the veil of night*
> *Coming for the cursed*
> *We race against the light*

Daniel knew it was time to flee what had become a perilous situation, but he hesitated when the specter abruptly snapped an unearthly horsewhip, dispelling a sinuous trail of fire that parted the mist surrounding the horse and carriage to reveal something Daniel had failed to notice, until now.

"My father's grave." He slumped against the tree in despair. "You're at the foot of my father's grave."

Suddenly, everything made perfect sense. The specter was a harvester, and he was after Daniel's father's soul.

With that knowledge, despair turned to desperation, and Daniel mustered the courage to step out of hiding and face the harvester who maintained a perfectly postured position high upon his carriage. The air grew colder and colder as Daniel eased closer and closer to the carriage, silently counting each arduous footstep, until coming to a stop on his thirteenth count. Now, near enough to get a detailed look at the specter's outer garments, the entity's face remained a featureless void, hidden beneath the hood of a black cloak that draped his thin frame.

"Are you a harvester? A collector?" Daniel bravely called out, his heart pounding like a jackhammer. "Are you after my father's soul?"

A moment of unsettling silence lingered as Daniel awaited a reply, only to be answered with another verse of the harvester's sinister song:

> *We are the collectors*
> *Collecting what is due*
> *We are the collectors*
> *Our harvest must ensue*

I hold a contract binding
An inescapable fey
A thousand years till ceasing
A debt you must repay

As the last word of the verse echoed, the specter reached into his cloak and pulled out a scroll that fell open in a flash of fire.

"The contract." The harvester's deep, cavernous voice was terrifying. "The blood of blood to pay." He pointed a bony finger at Daniel.

Daniel, glimpsing the harvester's skeletal face, stumbled backward with paralyzing fright.

"The blood of blood to pay," the harvester repeated.

Fearing his meaning, Daniel trembled. "You were never after my father's soul, were you?" he dared to ask. "You lured me out here as a clever trap, didn't you? It's *my* soul you want." He pressed his fingers against his chest. "MY SOUL!"

The harvester answered with a final refrain just as the eclipse reached totality, turning the moon blood red:

We are the collectors
Collecting what is due
We are the collectors
We come to collect...YOU!

With the snap of his whip that wrapped Daniel's body in fire, Daniel fell dead.

***

The following morning, Dawn and Cathy found Daniel's lifeless body in the cemetery, lying atop his father's grave. Gripped in his hand was a contract singed by fire and branded with three words:

PAID IN FULL.

THE COLLECTORS

Words and Music by
S.L. Claytor

1. We are the col-lec - tors___ Co - llec - ting what is due___
2. We are the col-lec - tors___ Co - llec - ting what is due___
3. We are the col-lec - tors___ Co - llec - ting what is due___
4. We are the col-lec - tors___ Co - llec - ting what is due___

We are the col-lec - tors___ Our har - vest must en - sue___
We are the col-lec - tors___ Our har - vest must en - sue___
We are the col-lec - tors___ Our har - vest must en - sue___
We are the col-lec - tors___ Our har - vest must en - sue___

The har - vest moon has ri - sen A har - bin - ger of fate
The migh - ty orb is blee - ding We en - ter now to reap
We tra - vel in the dark - ness Be-neath the veil of night
I hold a con - tract bin - ding An in - e - scap - able fey

[1. - 3.]

The full - est moon of ma - ny We wait to storm the gate
The bless - ed blood is ca - lling And what we take, we keep
Co - ming for the cur - sed We race a - gainst the light
A thou - sand years till cea - sing A debt you must re - pay

[4.]

We are the col-lec - tors___ Co - llec - ting what is due__

We are the col-lec - tors__ We come__ to__ co - llect__ YOU!

Vanderstein Castle.

"I hope 'The Collectors' didn't scare you too much. Every time I hear that ominous song, my cold bones shiver. Let this be a warning to you all, never sign a contract with the harvesters, because they *will* demand payment in full.

Sitting here, I've just become aware of a scratching sound within the wall behind me. Do you hear it? Yes, the noise is bothersome. I presume it must be a mouse, but in my experience, things are not always what they seem. Hopefully, by the time I read you another story, it will have gone away. This next ghostly tale is called 'The Haunting of Bedman's Creek.' I hope you enjoy it."

THE HAUNTING
OF BEDMAN'S CREEK

Wednesday, May 18.

The sun had just touched upon the western horizon as eleven-year-old Dylen Smith and his father, Mike, rounded the bend of a sleepy oxbow while river fishing. Moving against a choppy current in a 16-foot jon boat, Mike slowed to a trolling speed as they approached the mouth of Bedman's Creek.

"It's getting late, Dad." Dylen felt a sudden flood of apprehension. "I'd rather not go up the creek this close to dark."

Ominous shadows fell over the entrance of the narrow waterway, cast from overhanging trees that hugged the creek's steep bank. Overgrown shrubs and a canopy of interwoven vines, reminiscent of a jungle, created an illusion of entering a tunnel.

"We won't go far. Just to the old bridge." Mike headed into the creek, despite his son's reservations, dodging branches that crowded the gloomy passageway.

"This creek is creepy at night." Dylen ducked to avoid a large spiderweb that stretched the width of the creek. "That was close." He glanced back. "That is one big spider."

"A golden silk orb-weaver," Mike told him. "A banana spider."

Consumed by a sense of dread, Dylen sat down next to his dad and stared at the eerie view ahead, tuning in on the forlorn hoot of an owl in the near distance. "It's getting cold." He shivered, suddenly aware of a drastic drop in temperature, and rubbed his arms to brush off the unexpected chill. "This is weird for this time of year." His breath fogged when he spoke.

Glancing up at the treetops that swayed to a doleful moan, Dylen's uneasiness turned to utter fear when a faint, drawn-out whisper emanated from the woodsy bank on his left and rode on a gust of wind.

"One." The word was distinct, possessing a cold, unearthly tone.

"Did you hear that? I think someone is watching us." Dylen visually searched the dark bank, pretty sure he detected movement, but it was hard to distinguish what was there...what might be looking back.

"I didn't hear anything." Mike showed no concern. "There are a lot of animals scurrying around these woods. Squirrels. Raccoons. Armadillos." He maneuvered the boat past a fallen cabbage palm that half-blocked the waterway.

"It wasn't an animal." No one could convince Dylen otherwise. He was certain of what he'd heard and feared that someone, or something other than a forest animal, was following them along that shadowy bank. "Let's turn around, Dad. Please. I have a feeling something bad is about to happen."

"Don't be ridiculous, Dylen. There's nothing in these woods at night that isn't here during the day." Mike kept going. "I told you, we'll go as far as the old bridge."

Reaching the widest point of the creek known as Blind Bend, where the waterway ballooned to a span of at least thirty feet, the creek made a sharp left turn before bottlenecking back to its original narrow course.

"I heard a whisper, Dad," Dylen divulged exactly what he'd heard. "It wasn't an animal. It didn't even sound human. You've fished Bedman's Creek a lot over the years, have you ever experienced anything strange? Could it be haunted?"

"You know I don't believe in such nonsense." Mike continued to follow the winding waterway that gradually constricted as they moved deeper inland.

"What was that?" Dylen scrambled to his feet, startled by a loud splash near the bank.

"Probably an alligator." Mike cut the engine lever to neutral. "I'd say it was a big one."

The small boat rocked in the wake of the splash.

"Maybe." Dylen visually scanned the bank. "Wait. Someone's over there. Do you see those two people?" He caught sight of two dark, featureless figures that appeared to be children, their silhouetted forms barely perceptible. "They look like shadow kids."

Before Mike could respond, the two figures faded away, disappearing into the dark, shadow-laden surroundings.

Dylen then heard a second whisper, only this time there were two disembodied voices riding on a gust of wind.

"Two." The drawn-out word was faint but clear.

Dylen's blood ran cold. "You must have heard that." He didn't understand how his father could remain so calm.

"I heard...something," Mike admitted. "Probably just the wind blowing through the trees. There's always a logical explanation."

"It wasn't the wind, Dad. There are strange shadow kids out here with us. First, one of them whispered 'One'. And just now, right after seeing the two figures on the bank, I heard them whisper 'Two.'"

"There are no such things as shadow kids, Dylen." Mike returned the drifting boat to idle speed and continued along their serpentine course.

"Please, Dad. We need to get out of here." Dylen feared a point of no return, afraid that every inch they continued to move along that haunted creek, lessened their chances of escaping.

At that moment, the silhouetted beings appeared a third time on the bank, next to the remnants of an old dock.

"The shadow kids are back. And now there are three of them," Dylen alerted his dad.

"Three." The shadow kids' voices simultaneously chimed a third drawn-out whisper that caused Dylen to shudder with fear.

Mike glanced toward the bank. "The wind is really howling...making some strange sounds."

"That was not the wind, it's the shadow kids, and this time they said 'three.'"

"You're making me jumpy with all this nonsense." Mike continued along their course.

"Why won't you believe me? They're following us along the bank right now. Look, Dad. Can't you see them?" Dylen pointed. "Please, tell me you see them."

"Stop it, Dylen. What you're seeing is nothing more than play of light and shadows. You're seeing things that aren't there." Mike kept his eyes peeled on the course ahead. "We're just about at the bridge. We'll do a little fishing and then we'll head back."

Dylen watched in paralyzing fear as the three shadow kids continued to follow along the bank, his heart pounding harder and faster as Mike steered the boat toward an old wooden bridge.

"Well, we made it. Toss me that rope, and I'll tie the boat off." Mike pointed toward the bow.

He shut off the boat motor and waited while the swift-moving current carried them beneath the structure. Upon exiting the opposite side of the bridge, he quickly lassoed a cross support and secured the boat in place.

"They're watching us, Dad." Dylen broke his momentary silence. "Right there." He pointed toward the bank. "They want something."

"We're not going to get any fishing done until I prove to you that there is nothing over there." Mike reached into a storage compartment and pulled out a spotlight. Shining its bright beam of light onto the bank, he immediately drew in a quick breath. "What-what are those things?" he stammered in disbelief. "I'm sorry, Dylen, I should have believed you. I see them now."

"We need to get out of here, and fast," Dylen stressed the urgency. "If it's not already too late."

Mike quickly untied the boat and started the motor. "I don't know what those things are, but we're not sticking around a minute longer to find out. Hold on tight. We're getting out of here."

Speeding away, Dylen's blood turned icy cold when a fourth shadow kid suddenly materialized on top of the bridge and glared down at them with glowing red eyes.

"Hurry, Dad!" Dylen yelled, overcome by the worst fear he had ever experienced when the menacing figure roared the word 'four' and bolted from the bridge, joining the other three shadow kids in pursuit along the bank. "They're chasing us. There are four of them now."

It didn't take long to reach the remnants of the old dock, where once again, a menacing whisper echoed from the bank.

"Three." The ominous word rang louder and deeper than before.

The hair on the back of Dylen's neck stood on end.

"They're getting closer."

Mike expertly maneuvered the boat along the narrow, twisting course at a remarkable speed, but the shadow kids continued to close in on them in aggressive pursuit.

"Two." A second ghastly whisper drifted from the woodsy bank as they neared Blind Bend.

"Hurry, Dad!" Dylen watched in terror as the shadow kids shape-shifted from humanlike forms to monsterlike forms. "They're catching up with us, and they're definitely not human." He kept his eyes peeled on what were no longer shadow kids, but shadow creatures.

Mike struggled to maintain speed and control against a fierce and sudden squall. "This windstorm came out of nowhere."

"They're trying to stop us. Just keep going, Dad. Whatever you do, don't stop."

Barely staying ahead of their nightmarish pursuers, Mike had just dodged the fallen cabbage palm that half-blocked the waterway, when a third whisper echoed on a howling gust of wind.

"One." The ghastly whisper was the deepest and most fearsome by far.

Dylen watched in horror as the creatures grew closer, and closer, until practically parallel with the boat. "We're not going to make it." His gaze locked on the red-eyed shadow creature, fearing a terrible, inescapable fate.

"We're almost there." Mike made a mad dash for the mouth of the creek, fighting against an ever-strengthening windstorm.

"Were not going to make it." Dylen feared that the small boat might overturn at any moment.

Now, only mere feet from the mouth of Bedman's Creek, the red-eyed shadow creature released a piercing cry and lunged toward the boat at the exact moment Dylen and Mike exited the waterway.

"No!" Dylen yelled and dove to the floor, thinking this was to be a grizzly end for him and his dad.

"We made it." Mike glanced back at the creek. "That thing just exploded into a cloud of black mist, like it struck some invisible barrier."

"The shadow creatures...they're gone?" Dylen got up off the floor just in time to spot an oncoming boat. "Look out, Dad!"

Mike immediately cut the engine down to idle speed, watching as a bass boat approached, driven by a man dressed in red and black flannel. As the boat drew nearer, Dylen saw that a second person was onboard, trolling from the stern—a blonde-headed boy around his own age of eleven, wearing a Nike jacket and cap.

"Hello." The man waved as they slowly passed by.

"Did you have any luck in the creek? Are the fish biting?"

"Stay out of Bedman's Creek," Mike warned the stranger. "We just barely escaped some kind of shadow creatures. I know it sounds crazy, but it's true."

The man laughed. "Good joke. Trying to keep the good fishing spots to yourself, huh?"

"It's no joke," Mike called out to the man. "Trust me. There really are shadow creatures in that creek."

The man laughed again. "You better come up with a better story than 'shadow creatures' if you want to scare people away from the good spots."

"No. It's the truth," Mike tried to convince the man who continued idling toward the mouth of the creek. "Stay out of Bedman's Creek. If you go in there, you *will* regret it," he yelled out one final warning.

Dylen could hear the man and boy laughing as they entered the mouth of the creek. "You did warn them, Dad."

"Yeah." Mike sighed. "They were warned." He looked at Dylen. "They're on their own. We're going home." He shifted their engine into high gear and sped away.

As they rode, Dylen wondered what the shadow creatures actually were and why they were haunting Bedman's Creek. It was a dark mystery he knew he would probably never solve, because he had no intention of ever entering the mouth of Bedman's Creek again. Day or night. Never again.

***

The next afternoon, Dylen and his parents were having dinner at the dining room table, watching the local news on a TV that was viewable from the family room.

"Dad." Dylen suddenly dropped his fork. "Do you hear that news report? They're talking about two people missing since last night, a man and a boy whose last known location was fishing the river in a bass boat."

Mike stared at the TV, listening as the reporter continued her story and gave a description of the missing man and boy.

Eugene Millard was last seen wearing a red and black flannel shirt. His son, Matthew, age eleven, was wearing a Nike jacket and cap. If you have any information regarding their whereabouts, please call (xxx) xxx-xxxx.

Dylen's eyes grew wide when the missing duo's pictures appeared on the screen. "That's them, Dad. That's the man and boy we saw yesterday."

"It sure is," Mike confirmed in low spirits. "They should have listened."

"Your Dad told me what happened," Susan,

Dylen's mother, said. "I never believed in the haunting of Bedman's Creek...until now."

"What haunting?" Dylen was eager to know.

"Well, throughout the years it has been told that four shadow kids inhabit the creek, but they seldom appear to the living," Susan told him. "When they do make an appearance, they are heard calling out numbers from various spots along the bank of the creek, beginning on the count of one and continuing until a red-eyed shadow creature appears on the count of four. When that final red-eyed creature appears, a chase is initiated, and if their prey is caught before escaping the creek, the victims are snatched through the watery depths and into the netherworld."

"Why do they count to four?" Dylen was curious.

"According to legend, it is a game that the shadow kids play. They are said to guard four bases that are positioned along the creek, calling out each base as it is passed. Then, when their opponent reaches the fourth base, which is alleged to be the old bridge, the red-eyed shadow creature appears and yells 'four,' setting a cat and mouse chase into motion."

"That's exactly what happened to us." Dylen could hardly believe it was all just a game. A horrible, horrifying game. "And they almost caught us."

"Very few people have been lucky enough to win

the game and survive the haunting of Bedman's Creek," Susan said. "I can't imagine the shadow kids like to lose."

"No. Probably not." Dylen recalled the fierce predators. "We were lucky."

"Very lucky," Mike concurred. "We managed to outrun them, but we were only mere seconds away from being dragged down through the murky water and into the netherworld."

"Yep, it was a close call." Dylen would never forget the terrifying experience. "We played the shadow kids' game and won. Sadly, I can't say the same for Eugene and Matthew Millard, who apparently weren't so lucky."

Dylen imagined the duo trapped in a dark, grim netherworld with many other ill-fated victims who preceded them. For, like his mom said, very few people have been lucky enough to win the game and survive...the haunting of Bedman's Creek.

Vanderstein Castle.

"Unfortunately, while I told that last story, whatever is scratching within the wall has multiplied in number. I understand your concern, but please don't go. If you'll give me a moment, I will call an exterminator to assess the situation before it escalates any further. Luckily, I have a business card for just such a predicament."

The host holds up a card and reads it aloud.

"For infestations big or small, Roger Felis kills them all. For nighttime appointments or emergencies call (xxx) xxx-xxxx.

Roger sounds like the perfect exterminator for the job. If you'll excuse me for a moment, I'm going to step over to the next room and give him a call. I won't be long."

The host leaves his guests alone in the dim, dusty

library for five unnerving minutes with the lights continually threatening to cast them into utter darkness at any given moment.

"Roger was out on another call, but I left a message and expect a return call soon. Now, regarding that last story, 'The Haunting of Bedman's Creek,' it brings to mind an experience I had near that very creek when I was a boy. You see, there was this tree—the old buzzard tree."

THE OLD BUZZARD TREE

I once saw a tree, a very big tree,
A menacing tree—the old buzzard tree;
It stood by the water, a shivery sight,
All covered with buzzards, it gave me a fright.

I shuddered inside, and my blood ran cold,
Recalling a warning my grandmother told:
"Beware of the eerie old buzzard tree,
Do not go near it, please listen to me.

For there is a ghost, a tricky ol' ghost,
Bound 'neath the tree, he longs for a host.

The buzzards keep watch for passersby,
In sinister service till the day they die.

What menacing mood the earth doth spawn
When his cries ascend from the great beyond,
To lure you near and snare a host—
A wicked scheme of a villainous ghost.

Should ever you near the old buzzard tree,
I beg you once more, please listen to me:
Run for your life if the buzzards attack;
Ignore the ghost's cries, and never look back."

I feared the old tree. I feared the ol' ghost.
I feared the grave threat of becoming his host.
I shuddered once more, and I started to pray,
When an army of buzzards all peered my way.

Then came a fierce cry, and I covered my ears.
I tried not to listen; I trembled with fear.
At that very moment the buzzards took flight,
'Twas an ominous sight that tripled my fright.

I turned and I ran with all my might,
Fleeing the grasp of my spine-chilling plight.
That tricky ol' ghost was after a host,

And I was the host being chased by the ghost.

A cyclone of buzzards then darkened the sky,
With great trepidation, I thought I might die;
But I just kept running, I never looked back,
Till the vortex of buzzards withdrew their attack.

Thanks to my grandma, I outran that ghost,
Knowing he sought to make me his next host.
Now, I pass on this warning that she gave to me:
Stay far, far away from the old buzzard tree.

For there is a tree, a very big tree,
A menacing tree—the old buzzard tree.
It stands by the water, a shivery sight,
All covered with buzzards,
        IT WILL FILL YOU WITH FRIGHT!

Vanderstein Castle.

"I still have nightmares about that tree. If you ever see it, take my advice and stay far, far away, because you may not run fast enough to escape that tricky ol' ghost. Fortunately, I am a fast runner.

As I said before the poem, the exterminator should return my call soon, so while we wait, I'll read another story. This one is called 'The Curse of Campsite 13.'"

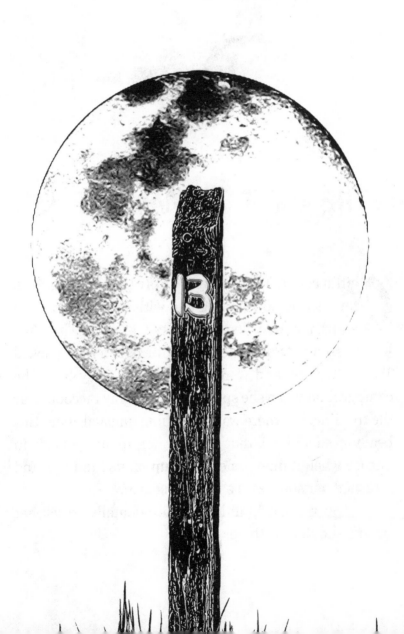

THE CURSE OF CAMPSITE 13

aitlin couldn't wait to get to Fort DeSoto State Park for a weekend camping trip with her parents, Tom and Lana, and her older sister, Ashley. They had just crossed the Sunshine Skyway Bridge in their packed Toyota Tacoma and were only minutes away from the campground when she spotted a furry, gray raccoon near the tree line. But there was something unusual about this beady-eyed animal that caused her to jump back in unease when it unexpectedly sat up on its hind legs and returned her stare with a menacing grin.

"Sorry, Ash." Caitlin had accidentally struck her sister's shoulder with her elbow.

"What is wrong with you?" Ashley snapped in irritation.

"Did you see that raccoon?" Caitlin motioned. "It was...weird."

"You'll see a lot of those masked, striped-tailed bandits around the park." Tom laughed. "I recall your Mom and I saw quite a few when camping here years ago."

"This will be a good experience for you girls." Lana glanced back at Caitlin and Ashley. "Your first camping trip."

"We're here." Caitlin called attention to a sign marking the camp entrance.

"Finally. I didn't think this ride was ever going to end." Ashley straightened from a slouched position as the truck rolled to a stop in front of the park office.

"I'll get us checked in." Tom got out, stretched his legs, and aimed for the office.

Caitlin stood next to the truck and gazed on a small cove where numerous boats lined a rocky shoreline. Intrigued, she headed toward the cove and sat on a bench shaded by several tall cabbage palms. She had only been sitting there for several seconds when a palm frond suddenly fell and narrowly missed hitting her.

"That was close."

She looked up in the tree and saw another

raccoon, this one staring down at her with a sinister-looking grin, as if responsible for the fallen frond.

Curious, she thought.

Just then, Lana called out from the truck, "Time to go."

Caitlin waved and called back, "I'm coming."

Before heading away, she glanced back up in the tree, but the raccoon had darted out of sight.

"There is definitely something strange about the animals here," she said and headed for the truck.

Following a winding road that meandered through the woodsy campground, they soon arrived at their assigned campsite.

"13?" Caitlin grimaced when she read the sign marking their site. "I don't like having campsite 13. Can't we get another site?"

"Don't be silly." Tom pulled into a small clearing amid cabbage palms and palmettos. "Since when are you so superstitious? Besides, it's the only spot they had left." He parked the truck and got out. "This is a great location. Right on the bay."

"I agree with Caitlin," Ashley said. "There's a reason campsite 13 was the only spot left. It's because of the legend. No one ever wants campsite number 13. Especially not on a full-moon night."

"How did you hear about that legend?" Lana

asked as she got out to help Tom remove four bikes from the bike rack.

"At school," Ashley answered. "My friend Tony told me about the curse of campsite 13 when he found out we were coming here."

"There's a legend...a curse? What did he tell you?" Caitlin wanted to know.

"Well," Ashley's lips stretched into a mischievous smirk, "long ago, on a full-moon night, a family was camping right here at campsite 13, in this very spot. Legend says that two brothers went to bed in their tent, but when morning came, it was discovered that one of the boys had vanished." Ashley dramatized the story. "They say the surviving boy went mad, claiming that wereraccoons had ripped through the tent and taken his brother in the middle of the night."

"Wereraccoons?" Caitlin recalled the sinister grin cast by the raccoon she'd seen in the cabbage palm by the cove.

"Yep." Ashley nodded. "And they always target campsite number 13."

"That's enough, Ashley." Lana called out from the back of the truck. "You're scaring your sister with that foolishness."

"Your mom's right," Tom seconded. "Now, both of you get out here and help us unload this truck. We need to pitch the tents before dark."

Caitlin opened her door, but she hesitated to get out when she heard a noise and caught a glimpse of gray fur from an animal scrambling up a nearby tree. She tried not to think of wereraccoons or the legend, but that was hard to do when the campsite 13 sign stood in open view as a constant reminder.

An hour later, Caitlin sat at a picnic table with her dad who was cooking hotdogs on a small grill. A mandarin sunset over the bay ushered in nightfall, and as darkness settled, she grew more and more unsettled at the thought of spending the night at campsite 13. She didn't want to believe the legend of the wereraccoons, but something just wasn't right about the raccoons in the park. They seemed downright menacing.

"Can you take this out to the large trashcans for me?" Tom tied up a bag of trash and handed it to Caitlin.

She reluctantly took the bag and inched toward the shadow-laden road, aiming for two trashcans that sat on the opposite side of the pavement. Reaching the trashcans, she lifted a lid, but jumped back with a start when a raccoon leaped from the can and landed mere inches from her. She slowly backed away, terrified that the animal might attack, but it just stopped and stared at her with glowing red eyes.

"You only have a stripe over one eye." Caitlin observed the unusual characteristic of this particular raccoon. "You're a half-masked bandit."

She then shuddered when the animal responded with a snarl-like grin that showed its unnaturally long, jagged teeth, never expecting what happened next.

"Lucky number 13." The raccoon spoke in a boy's voice.

Struck with all-consuming fear, Caitlin turned and bolted back to the picnic table where her dad was taking the hotdogs off the grill.

"Dad." She was short of breath. "I just saw another raccoon, and it spoke to me. It said, 'Lucky number 13.'"

"I was afraid that story your sister told might give you nightmares tonight, but I didn't think it would trouble you this much." Tom motioned for her to sit down at the table. "Trust me, there are no curses or wereraccoons. Nothing terrible is going to happen tonight just because we're staying in campsite 13."

At that moment, Lana and Ashley joined them at the table.

"Both tents are set up." Lana reached for a package of paper plates. "We should sleep comfortably."

"If we survive the night," Caitlin moaned, laying her head on the table.

Lana looked at her. "Is that story about the curse of campsite 13 troubling you?"

"It sure is," Tom answered. "But I just reassured her that there is nothing to be afraid of."

"I don't know, Caitlin. It's a full moon tonight, so you better keep an eye open." Ashley spoke in a ghostly voice. "Or the wereraccoons just might...getcha!" She jumped at her sister.

"Enough," Tom snapped. "I don't want to hear any more about wereraccoons."

Caitlin tried to ignore her sister, but she was certain of what she'd seen and heard. That raccoon spoke, and she was terror-stricken by what it said: "Lucky number 13."

The image of the raccoon's red eyes and sharp, jagged teeth kept reappearing in her mind. She couldn't help wondering if the animal would soon transform into something wicked; if the light of the full moon would soon turn it into a wereraccoon.

After dinner, Caitlin climbed into a tent she was sharing with her sister and settled down for the night. Separated from Ashley by a divider, she laid in the darkness and listened to the sounds of the night—frogs, cicadas, crickets, and various birds—too scared to sleep.

"It's getting cold." She called to Ashley, unnerved by a sudden drop in temperature and the onset of a howling wind that whipped the tent flaps with such force that she worried the tent might blow over. She then shot upright when she heard a clawing sound. "Ashley, do you hear that clawing?"

Ashley untied the divider separating their rooms and poked her head through. "Quiet down. You're going to wake Mom and Dad."

"What is that clawing?" Caitlin was too afraid to unzip the tent door and look outside.

"It's probably raccoons," Ashley whispered. "Do you want to know why the raccoons only target site 13? Why it's cursed?"

"Not really." Caitlin wished her sister would stop talking about the curse.

Ashley continued anyway. "A hundred years ago, in this very spot, a witch cursed a boy for stealing from her by turning him into a wereraccoon. Since then, on full-moon nights, they say he appears with a group of other wereraccoons—children he has changed into wereraccoons over the years—targeting kids that are the age he was when he was cursed...your age."

"I don't want to hear anymore." Caitlin covered her ears.

"He only claims kids that stay at site 13, right here, where he was cursed. And according to the legend, he can be recognized by his half mask; he only has a stripe over one eye."

Caitlin gasped, and her eyes grew wide. "I've seen that raccoon; it spoke to me in a boy's voice. It said, "Lucky number 13."

"Sure it did." Ashley rolled her eyes.

"I really saw him, Ashley. I really did."

"Well, if that's true, then you better beware, because all it takes is one scratch from a wereraccoon's claw to turn you into one of them. So, don't let them get too close." Ashley withdrew into her room. "Sweet dreams, little sis." She shut and retied the divider.

Caitlin, livid with her sister for intentionally scaring her, was now more afraid than ever. Lying awake, she kept thinking about the half-masked raccoon, fairly certain that he was the same wereraccoon from the legend—the boy who'd been cursed by the witch a hundred years earlier.

"It has to be him." She spoke under her breath. "How many talking, half-masked raccoons could there possibly be?"

Plagued by fear, she fought to stay awake, but soon exhaustion caught up with her and she drifted off to sleep. She wasn't sure how long she'd been sleeping when she suddenly jolted awake, shaken by the sound an animal chattering nearby.

"I'm never going camping again." She reached for her cell phone and checked the time—precisely 1:00 a.m. "Go away, raccoons." She pulled her blanket up under her chin, shuddering when the chattering sounds appeared to grow closer. And closer.

At that moment, a shadow appeared along the tent wall in front of her—the silhouette of a raccoon. Then, a second shadow appeared, followed by a third shadow, and a fourth, until there was at least a dozen.

"Wereraccoons," she uttered in a trembling whisper.

With eyes wide with fright, she watched the silhouettes grow taller and taller as they shape-shifted into hunchbacked creatures the height of a person. Shivering at the sight of what appeared to be outlines of long fangs and claws, she feared that the monsters might rip through the tent fabric and snatch her away at any moment. Then, she heard something that made her blood run bitter cold.

"Lucky number 13," a boy's voice whispered.

Caitlin instantly recognized the voice of the half-masked bandit and knew what he was after...who he was after. Seized in a petrified state, her pulse sped faster and faster when the wereraccoons all appeared to simultaneously turn and look in her direction. They inched closer. And closer. And closer. Until....

A horrific scream rang out.

"Caitlin?" Ashley untied the divider and peeked into her sister's room. "CAITLIN!" she cried out in horror, but it was too late. Much too late.

***

The police arrived and initiated a search for Caitlin, finding the tent shredded, suspecting an animal attack. But Ashley knew what had happened, rambling on about wereraccoons and the curse of campsite 13, desperately trying to make her parents and the authorities believe her.

"You don't understand. She's still here. She's been turned into one of them," Ashley told them. "He only targets campsite 13. He changes kids that are the age he was when he was cursed. You must believe me. I saw the wereraccoons. I saw *him*—the cursed one—the half-masked bandit. He is real. The curse of campsite 13 is real. IT'S ALL REAL!"

After that night, Ashley was never the same again, and sadly, Caitlin was never found. But campsite 13 is still there, and someday, on a full-moon night, the half-masked bandit will strike again. It is the curse of campsite 13.

Vanderstein Castle.

"Wereraccoons. Do you suppose that's what is making all that noise inside the wall behind me? You look concerned. Don't worry, I'm only joking."

Ring, ring, ring.

"That is probably the exterminator returning my call. I'll be right back."

The host steps away.

"Please excuse the brief delay. That was indeed the return call I was expecting. Roger Felis is on his way, and the sooner the better, for the clawing is spreading and growing louder by the minute. By the sound of it, there must now be five or six creatures scurrying around in this wall. But since there is nothing any of us can do except wait for assistance, we might as well enjoy another story. This next tale is about a doctor who lived in South

Florida in the 1800s who resorted to cruel and desperate measures to attain something that no mortal man is meant to have. It is called 'A Tooth for a Tooth.'"

A TOOTH FOR A TOOTH

I walked the north bank of the Caloosahatchee River that bordered my 800-acre estate several miles east of Fort Myers. I paused at a sharp bend in the river, where an aged cabbage palm leaned toward the water, having spotted a familiar alligator sunning on the shell-littered bank. The gator, realizing my presence, suddenly spun about and released a threatening growl.

"Chogan." I recognized the creature by a tattoo that covered the right side of his leathery face, where the skin was marbled with human-like flesh. Yes, that tattoo gave his identity away, along with those large brown eyes that stared up at me with utter hatred.

"Accept what you are, Chogan. You may no longer be human, but the serum I used to alter your DNA was infused with an ingredient that will drastically lengthen your lifespan by generations. You will live a very long life."

I knew that Chogan understood my words when he hissed and held an aggressive stance.

"I'm sorry, Chogan. I admit, things did not turn out as I had hoped, but this failed attempt has not stopped my research."

Keeping a close eye on Chogan, I carefully backed away and returned to the main house—a twelve-room, two-story mansion wrapped in open verandas and supported by impressive columns that stretched from the ground to the second level roof. Inside, a patient suffering from consumption occupied an upstairs bedroom. The perfect timing of his arrival three weeks earlier from a nearby fort had allowed me the means to continue my research, for I was in desperate need of a new subject.

Entering the young man's room, I approached the patient, and saw terror in his eyes. "I understand why you fear me." I pulled a vial from my coat pocket and prepared a syringe for injection. "But my treatment will save your life." I administered the injection. "You will never be as you were, but I can guarantee a long, long life."

This was the third injection I had given this particular subject, and the final effects were visibly apparent. His pointed teeth and sharp claws that emerged during his first week were just the beginning of what was becoming an agonizing transformation from human to reptilian.

"I should pity you, but I'm afraid I feel no compassion. You might say I'm mad, that I have no moral sense, but everything I have done has been in the interest of science."

I examined the man's physical mutations, observing a gradually protruding snout, knowing that a tail would soon follow. His hair had fallen out, and his skin was now peeling from his flesh as it transitioned from human tissue to bony reptilian scales. This, of course, was an unfortunate side effect, which continued to be a repeated obstacle, but I would never give up my quest for immortality.

Leaving the room, I retreated to my lab and reviewed my notes. Sixteen months of research filled the pages of a green, hardbound journal documenting my journey from day one to present time. At the start of my research, I had gained the trust of a neighboring native tribe with whom I resided for nearly a year while garnering their tribal secrets of herbal medicines, the craft of mixing potions, and their ancient rituals of spells and magic. However, the shaman—a gifted wizard—refused to divulge all of his secrets, stating that mortal men were not meant to live forever.

But I was determined to conquer death, and one evening, without his knowledge, I followed the shaman to the edge of the river, where I hid and spied as he summoned a strange reptilian creature from the depths of the water. The reptile was large—at least twelve feet long—resembling an alligator, yet it stood taller and had a uniquely rounded head shape with humanlike features. Then, to my amazement, it spoke. I could scarcely make out the conversation, but I heard the gator creature mention an ancient pact with the natives, commenting on the fact that it had outlived numerous generations of the shaman's tribe. Then, before returning to the river, the creature gifted the shaman with a fresh tooth.

It was a remarkable revelation to learn that this creature either aged very slowly or was immortal. And what power did that tooth possess that the shaman carefully placed it in a small, leather pouch? I had to know at any cost, so I stole it.

"Through trial and error, I will succeed. I am very close to discovering the right formula. So very close."

After jotting down the day's notes, I replaced the book on the shelf and reached for a small pouch that suspended from a cord around my neck. I removed the remaining portion of the tooth and ground it into a fine powder. This was the last of it.

"My final chance to get it right." I carefully placed the powder in a vial and set it aside in preparation for my next attempt, knowing I'd need a new test subject soon.

Several long hours passed as I worked tirelessly to perfect my formula, but exhaustion eventually forced me to retire to my room, where the shaman appeared to me in a dream.

"You've angered the spirits," he warned. "Immortality is not meant for mortal men." He drew closer and closer. "A tooth for a tooth in penance." I felt his breath upon my face. "A tooth for a tooth."

At that moment, the sound of a loud crash awakened me from my nightmare, and I rushed to investigate, finding my test subject stumbling out of his room and into the hallway. Much to my surprise, his complexion appeared to be reverting to its original state of human flesh; and although he was still quite weak, he showed drastic overall improvement from mere hours earlier.

"The formula...it's working. I've finally found the right mixture and dosage." I could hardly believe my own words, ecstatic to learn that the serum I had administered to him was successfully altering his DNA in a positive way by healing and renewing his body. "I have finally done it!" I threw my head back and waved my fists in the air, unable to contain my enthusiasm.

Until now, my formulations had always resulted in a reptilian dominance over human DNA, but this time my subject's human DNA appeared to be maintaining dominance. This was a momentous scientific achievement.

"What immoral thing have you done to me?" The soldier demanded to know.

I lowered my arms and looked at him. "I've given you immortality. You will live a very long life. You are my success."

"You've used me for your wicked experiments." The man glared with contempt. "You are mad!" He aimed for the stairs. "I'm getting out of here. Now!"

I rushed to block his escape. He was my success, and I could not allow him to leave. So, I wrestled him back into his room and locked him inside.

Eager to start my own treatment, I hurried to the lab, reached for the vial containing the last of the ground tooth, and duplicated the exact serum I had used on the soldier. I then prepared a syringe for injection—one of three I would need over the course of three weeks—and following a moment of hesitation, I administered my first self-injection.

"There is no turning back now," I told myself. "It is done."

Over the course of the first week, I encountered a few expected side effects: First, I developed a taste for live food and an urge to hunt. Then came the loss of my teeth, which were replaced by pointed alligator teeth. But it was the end of the second week that brought a much more painful transformation, for it was then that my skin began shedding, and the shape of my body began taking on major physical reptilian characteristics. The agony of twisting bones and ripping muscles was almost unbearable, but in the end, my prize to come would be well worth the suffering I was currently enduring. I knew I could anticipate the same successful results as that of my test subject, who was not only fully cured of his consumption, but now appeared human again; however, something about him did not feel entirely human, which I admit troubled me.

Standing in front of a mirror, my frightening reptilian reflection gave me pause, but I had no choice but to proceed with my final injection. I reminded myself that in the end, I would achieve a lifespan that multiplied that of a mortal man. I had no idea how long I would actually live—for an accurate determination of time was impossible to calculate—but I trusted I would be walking the earth for a long time to come.

Just then, an abrupt pounding shook the walls, and I rushed to investigate, finding the source of the noise resided within the room that held my prisoner. I stood at the door, unnerved by the sound of grating against wood—a familiar sound I had heard before.

"No." I scrambled back from the door when a deep, guttural growl rumbled. "It cannot be."

Fearing the worst, I mustered the courage to unlock and open the door, momentarily stunned by the sight of a mutant gator-like creature thrashing about the room.

"Nooo. How can this be? The formula was working." I was devastated by the cruel deception my formula had played on me. "It. Was. Working." I cried out with clenched fists and fell onto my knees, knowing I was doomed.

Slumped over in a state of self-pity, I suddenly straightened when the gator creature hissed and charged past me. I scrambled to my feet and chased after him, watching as he slithered down the stairs and broke through a first-floor window. Moving fast, he disappeared in the direction of the river. There was nothing I could do to stop him, nor would it have mattered, for my cursed fate was sealed. Not only was my time as a man sorely limited, but the last of the ground tooth was gone, making me the final test subject.

"It was all for nothing."

As I stood there, I reflected on something I had told the soldier: "You will never be as you were, but I can guarantee a long, long life."

How ironic, the turn of events. How dark and doomfully ironic.

***

Several months later.

Late one evening, I crawled from the water in reptilian form and met my shaman neighbor on the bank of the Caloosahatchee River.

"We have a new visitor who has come to learn our ways, but I fear he is not trustworthy," the shaman told me in a hushed voice. "He thinks I am not aware of him following me, but what he does not realize is that I have purposely led him here."

"The way you once led me here when I stayed with your tribe?" The realization angered me. "You tricked me."

"It was a test. If one does not take the tooth, they are worthy of knowledge. If one takes the tooth, they suffer the wrath of the spirits." The shaman showed no remorse. "There are others living with the curse, some who are ages old, as you discovered upon following me that fateful evening. I warned you, men are not meant to live forever. Immortality is not meant—"

"...for mortal men." I finished his sentence. "I was certain I had discovered the right formulation, but I was mistaken."

"Even if you had, the spirits would not have allowed you to succeed," the shaman divulged. "Immortality was never achievable."

"There's something I don't understand, since I can talk, why can't the individuals I changed through experimentation do the same?"

"Only those cursed by the spirits are left with the ability to speak, as well as retaining their human memories and emotions. It is all part of their punishment—to always remember how precious human life is—for you will always long for what you have lost."

"Immortality as a mutant. A monster. But I accept what I've become." I had no choice but to accept my curse.

"My people have always forged pacts with the toothies," the shaman told me. "We wish to coexist peaceably."

"Toothies." I chuckled. "That says it all, for it started and ended with a tooth."

The shaman nodded. "That is what led you to your

curse. And that is what I ask for now."

"You want one of my teeth?" I knew he had summoned me for a purpose.

"Yes. I ask for one tooth," the shaman requested. "What you stole, you must give back. A tooth for a tooth in penance."

"A tooth for a tooth. To test your new visitor, just as you once tested me." I understood.

"Yes. That is all I ask," the shaman said. "But I hope you will agree to a pact so that I may call upon you again from time to time."

"I'm not sure I'm willing to give up that many teeth." I needed my teeth to survive.

"When you willingly offer a tooth, another will grow back in its place," the shaman assured me.

"I really am a toothie." I chuckled again. "About the pact, what might I gain in return?"

"You will be granted protection by the spirits."

"Protection? From the very spirits that cursed me?" I couldn't help laughing at yet another ironic turn of events.

Agreeing to a pact, I played along with the deceptive undertaking to set the test in motion, feeling a hint of pity for the individual being tested. I knew what the prospect of immortality could drive a man to do. Especially a greedy, immoral man.

From that moment, the shaman spoke louder to ensure that the spy overheard. We spoke of the ancient pact, being sure to mention how I would outlive numerous generations of the shaman's tribe. Then, before returning to the river, I made my offering.

"A tooth for a tooth," I whispered, and in penance, granted the shaman one fresh tooth.

With the deed done, I crawled back into the rushing water and sank into the river's dark, murky depths. I didn't know if, or when, I would see the shaman again, but I knew I would outlive him and those to descend him. For being a cursed immortal toothie, my sentence had only just begun.

Vanderstein Castle.

"After hearing 'A Tooth for a Tooth' I suppose you'll now be leery of walking the banks of the Caloosahatchee River if you're ever in South Florida. If that is the case, I apologize, for that was never my intention. I'm sure you'd be perfectly safe walking the banks, but you should probably keep an eye out for those alligator creatures, on the off-chance I am wrong."

A bookshelf violently rattles, and everyone jumps.

"I sure hope the exterminator gets here soon to take charge of this situation. The clawing is quickly escalating, now spreading to the adjoining walls. Yes, it is somewhat disconcerting, but we must remain calm. So, let's keep our minds off the growing problem with another story. The name of this unnerving tale is 'Midnight Madness in the Sky.'"

MIDNIGHT MADNESS IN THE SKY

While on vacation in the Great Smoky Mountains, Renna Jones, a very shy sixteen-year-old girl, met seventeen-year-old Lenny, whose father managed the Bear Cave Mountain Cabin Lodgings where Renna's family was staying for a month. Lenny, an outgoing individual, looked the epitome of wild rebel, expressing his punk-fashion style with an abundance of leather, neon-blue spiked hair, and several facial piercings. Despite being polar opposites in style and personality, Renna was intrigued by Lenny and met him as often as possible. As the saying goes, opposites attract.

It was Thursday, October 12, and Lenny asked Renna if she would go on a date with him that evening to an amusement park called Midnight Madness in the Sky. Learning that the park was only open at night, with hours of operation from 10 p.m. to 2 a.m., Renna's parents would only permit her to go if accompanied by a chaperone—her older sister Jeanine—who was three years her senior.

So, with instructions to check in with their parents at midnight, the three teens departed the cabin lodgings around 8 o'clock, in route to Midnight Madness in the Sky.

Arriving at the amusement park ticket window a few minutes before 10 p.m., Renna discovered that Midnight Madness in the Sky sat atop a mountain, with chairlifts being the only means of reaching the park.

"It is literally 'in the sky,'" Jeanine said as she got in line to purchase park tickets.

Renna noticed the short line of visitors, having expected a crowd. "I wonder why there aren't more people here."

"It's early," Lenny told her. "It will get busier. In fact, come midnight, I predict utter madness."

"Hilarious." Jeanine rolled her eyes.

At the top of the hour, Renna, Lenny, and Jeanine

boarded a chairlift that slowly carried them up the mountain to Midnight Madness in the Sky. Carnival music grew louder as they neared their destination, boosting Renna's enthusiasm; however, when the park finally came into view and they exited the chairlift, she found the place lacking the bright lights and vibrant colors she expected from any fair, carnival, or amusement park.

"Come one, come all." A pale man dressed in full black greeted them as they entered the park. "Welcome to Midnight Madness in the Sky."

"This isn't quite what I expected." Renna was somewhat disappointed to find the park to be more of a traveling carnival with fair rides, fun houses, and game booths, than an actual amusement park.

"It's strange...kind of creepy," Jeanine said. "The carnies are all so pale. And look at how they're dressed in outlandish costumes. It's so weird. Is it a circus, a carnival, or a park?"

Renna shared her sister's unease. The park was downright menacing.

"It's all just for show." Lenny led them deeper into the park. "Let's hit the rides...have some fun."

With what appeared to be less than a hundred people touring the park, the next hour passed quickly as Renna, Jeanine, and Lenny moved from one ride to the next with little to no wait times. Then, deciding to explore more of the park, they wandered into a section that was dedicated to freak show acts such as a Transylvanian werewolf, a netherworld troll, and a two-headed dragon.

"Let's go in and see some of these," Lenny said with enthusiasm. "I'd really like to get a look at this Transylvanian werewolf."

"You know these creatures aren't real." Renna glanced over the disturbing artwork painted on the side of the trailer—dark illustrations that supposedly depicted what awaited inside.

"Come on," Lenny urged. "If this one fails to impress, then I promise, we'll skip the rest."

"It looks scary." Renna frowned. "But I guess I'll survive."

"Wait." Jeanine checked her watch. "It's almost midnight. I'd better call Mom and Dad and check in?"

Renna stood next to Jeanine as she placed the call, assuring their parents that they were having a good time.

"Let's go." Lenny hastened them off the phone.

Jeanine ended the call. "What's the rush?"

Lenny pointed to a sign and then tapped his watch. "The show starts at midnight."

"Have you noticed how busy this freak show alley has suddenly gotten?" Jeanine observed.

What had only moments before been a quiet section of the park had suddenly sprung to life with sideshow barkers appearing in front of each attraction, enticing people inside with their "Hurry, hurry, step right up!" spiels.

Looking around, Renna recognized many of their fellow visitors in the crowd, having seen them off-and-on since entering the park. She thought it odd how they had all ended up in the freak show area at the same time; and even more bizarre, at the stroke of midnight.

"Something about this doesn't feel right," Renna whispered to Jeanine. "It also just dawned on me that as of this very minute, it's Friday the 13th."

"It's time." Lenny headed into the Transylvanian werewolf attraction. "We better get inside."

Renna, unnerved by the creepy atmosphere, was not as eager as Lenny to step inside the trailer, but not wanting to disappoint her date, she and Jeanine reluctantly followed him past a sinister-looking barker and into the attraction where they were seated in a narrow room, facing a black stage. A sudden, blinding red light signaled the appearance of a thin, ghastly man dressed in an old-fashioned suit and black cape. He floated across the stage in a ghostly manner, his pallid face showing minimal expression as he talked about an age-old hatred between vampires and werewolves, an introduction followed by a story about a Transylvanian vampire family that had captured and enslaved a werewolf.

"This is the very werewolf you are about to encounter," the man claimed. "A magnificent, terrifying, hungry creature."

"I hate this," Renna whispered to Lenny, who grinned, loving every minute of the intense show.

A sudden clap of thundering sound effects filled the room, coinciding with disorienting flashing lights.

"I present to you the Transylvanian werewolf." The showman yanked the cover off the cage in a swift, dramatic movement.

Jeanine shrieked and grabbed Renna's hand. "That thing is real."

The caged seven-foot-tall canine creature released a bone-chilling howl and shook the iron bars of the cage with such intensity that Renna feared it might break free.

"Ok, I've seen enough. Lenny, get us out of here," Renna insisted.

"I'm afraid that's not going to happen." Lenny cast an evil grin, revealing fangs. "Contrary to what you said earlier, the creatures here are very real." He got up and walked onto the stage.

"No. This can't be happening." Renna visually searched for an exit, seeing no way out, not even the entrance where they had entered, for it had disappeared as if by magic. "You can't be a...."

"Yes, Renna, I am a vampire. Think about our time together. We have never met during the day...always at night. Everything should be obvious by now." Lenny sneered. "Midnight Madness in the Sky is run by the undead."

"Our parents know we're here," Jeanine reminded him.

Lenny laughed. "Come morning light we will be long gone. That's the beauty of a traveling carnival."

"Midnight Madness was never a real amusement park." Renna's voice trembled.

"It once was, but it closed down thirty years ago after a mass killing of more than fifty people," Lenny informed her. "I was here when it happened then, and I'm here now, as history repeats itself."

"Just like thirty years ago, you plan to kill everyone visiting the park tonight?" A chill swept down Renna's spine when several distant screams rang out, but she knew that nothing could be done to save those poor souls. "We were lured here so you and the other vampires can feed on us?"

"No, mortal child, you don't understand." The caped showman stood next to Lenny. "This is a celebration. This is the Midnight Feast," he said. "You're not here to feed us." He reached out a bony hand and unlatched the werewolf's cage. "We must feed our pets. Our many. Many. Precious. Pets."

As the werewolf lunged, Renna and Jeanine's bloodcurdling screams echoed, and soon all grew silent. Deathly silent.

***

Just before 8 a.m., a police car pulled up to the office at Bear Cave Mountain Cabin Lodgings where two detectives were met by Renna and Jeanine's parents, Mr. and Mrs. Jones.

"Hello. I'm Detective Ryan, and this is Detective Phillips. You reported two missing teens?"

"Yes, our daughters." Mr. Jones shook each detective's hand. "They went out last night with the lodge manager's son Lenny and never returned. We've been calling their cell phones for hours but get no answer."

"Have you spoken to the manger to see if he's heard from his son?" Detective Phillips inquired.

"We've been waiting for him." Mr. Jones held tightly to his distraught wife's hand. "We were told that he starts work at 8 a.m."

Detective Ryan checked his watch. "It's nearly that time. Let's step inside the office and see what we can find out."

Entering the front door, they came upon the manager arriving through a back entrance, and the detectives immediately questioned him to learn the whereabouts of his son Lenny. But to their astonishment, he insisted that he had no son named Lenny. He, in fact, claimed to have no children at all.

Mrs. Jones gasped. "If Lenny is not your son...who is he?"

The room momentarily fell silent.

"Where did the kids go last night?" Detective Phillips turned his questioning back on the Joneses.

"They said they were going to an amusement park called Midnight Madness in the Sky," Mr. Jones told him.

The manager suddenly stumbled backward. "That's not possible."

"What do you mean? What's wrong?" Mrs. Jones demanded to know.

The manager shook his head, saying nothing more.

"What are you not telling us," Mr. Jones pressed him for an answer.

"That amusement park," the manager finally broke his silence, "it was closed down over thirty years ago after a mass killing."

"Until we know more, there's no reason to panic,"

Detective Ryan told the Joneses. "However, I should inform you of something." He paused for several tense seconds. "Your missing persons call is but one of many we've received this morning," he confessed. "The station has been flooded with calls, and all of the missing people were said to have gone to Midnight Madness in the Sky."

"Wait." The manager raised a finger. "What did this boy, Lenny, look like?"

Mr. Jones did his best to describe Lenny's punk-rock style and blue spiked hair.

"I used to know someone who matches that description." The manager rushed to a cabinet and thumbed through some papers. "Yes, here it is." He handed Mr. Jones a flyer. "The Amazing Stefan Mondragon and son Lenny. I remember them from the old days, when I worked at the park."

"This is dated thirty years ago. This can't possibly be the same young man." Mr. Jones closely examined the flyer. "But it looks just like him."

"I believe it is him," the manager said. "Mondragon was a famous animal tamer, and he also ran a traveling sideshow that exhibited what was rumored to be real monsters. Word amongst the carnies quickly spread of his dark eccentricities, especially of his obsession with his monsters, which he referred to as his pets.

Mondragon and his show had teamed up with the owner of Midnight Madness in the Sky for a short time, but when disagreements arose, his clan pulled out, and the very next night, the massacre occurred. Now, you may think I'm crazy, but I've always believed Mondragon was responsible for that mass killing. I, myself, would have been killed if I had not missed work that night."

"We need to stick to the facts. I can't image that the mass killing thirty years ago has anything to do with what's happening now," Detective Ryan said.

"I wouldn't be so sure," the manager disagreed. "You see, Mondragon was not only an animal tamer and sideshow owner, he was also purported to be a vampire."

"That's ridiculous," Detective Ryan scoffed.

"To see the pale, skeletal man was reason enough to believe," the manager told him. "I imagine the officers you've sent up to the top of that mountain to investigate will find an area drenched with blood, but if the scene is anything like thirty years ago, there won't be much left of those missing folks to identify. I'm sorry, Mr. and Mrs. Jones, but if history has repeated itself, you can bet that any visitors at the park last night were led straight to the slaughter by Mondragon and his clan."

"No." Mrs. Jones burst into tears. "This can't be true." She didn't know what to believe.

"That's enough," Detective Ryan cautioned the

manager. "This nonsense is making matters worse."

"Could it be true?" Mr. Jones's gaze remained fixed on the flyer.

"Friday the 13th. The Midnight Feast at Midnight Madness in the Sky." The manager disregarded the detective's warning to drop the subject. "A carny once told me that Mondragon always threw a yearly feast for his beasts, a celebration he called the Midnight Feast, and that it always took place during the first hour of a Friday that fell on a 13th day. That, I believe, is what took place last night—the Midnight Feast."

No one interrupted the manager, for as crazy as it all sounded, it frighteningly made sense.

"It's over now," the manager continued, "but someday, I fear, Mondragon will return yet again. So, give warning to your friends and family, and remind them to pass this warning on to their descendants. Let them know to be wary of any new friends—especially a young man named Lenny—who may invite them to an amusement park on the eve of Friday the 13th. For should they ever accept his invitation, once they step foot atop that ill-fated mountain, they will never return from...Midnight Madness in the Sky.

Vanderstein Castle.

"Friday the 13th. That day used to always make me nervous, and after that last story, with good reason."

Knock. Knock. Knock.

"That must be the exterminator at the door. If you'll pardon the interruption, I'll show him in."

The host vacates the room and returns momentarily with the exterminator.

"I'm sorry that took so long. Say hello to Roger. He assures me he is going to resolve this predicament—whatever is invading the space within these walls—before I end up with a full infestation on my hands.

What was that, Roger? You say you need to go to the room below this one to fully assess the situation? Well, that would be the basement. I hope you don't mind going alone. I would accompany you, but as you can see,

I am entertaining guests."

The host shows Roger into the corridor and gives him directions to the basement.

"Just watch your step. The stairs can be tricky. And with the storm affecting the power, you could find yourself in total darkness down there at any given moment.

What? You say you have a light? Well, that's good. Yes, it looks like a very reliable light. Now, if you have things well in hand, I will get back to my guests."

The host steps back into the library.

"I apologize for the interruptions, but you understand the magnitude of the matter. The escalation of the clawing and gnawing within these walls has become impossible to ignore; but rest assured, Roger is a professional and should handle the case accordingly. So, with that assurance, let's move on to another story. This one is a real hair-raiser. It is called 'The Clown.'"

THE CLOWN

THE ASTONISHING CIRCUS OF ARAH! was in town, and Calvin, along with his friends Rebecca, Trina, and David, purchased tickets for a night of fun. They had just stepped through the entrance gate when Calvin came face-to-face with a character from his worst nightmares—a frightening, wide-mouthed clown dressed as a cowboy.

"I've got my eye on you." The clown pointed an index finger at his left eye.

Calvin darted past the clown and ran to the entrance of the big top. "I hate clowns. I really, really, hate them."

Rebecca, Trina, and David caught up with him.

"We know." Trina laughed. "I don't think you're ever going to get over your fear of clowns."

"I've seen that one before." Calvin remembered this particular clown from prior visits to the traveling circus.

He shuddered at the sight of his eerily familiar painted face, ball nose, and black ragdoll hair that appeared to have a life of its own, springing out in disarray beneath a brown, weathered cowboy hat. The thought of not being able to see the true identity of the person hiding beneath that colorful costume and makeup made his flesh crawl.

"We're seniors, for Pete's sake." David ridiculed his friend. "You need to get over this childish fear. You're eighteen-years-old. It's embarrassing to run away from clowns at our age."

"Ignore him, Calvin." Rebecca glared at David. "We know you've had this fear since we were kids."

"We're not kids anymore." David was unsympathetic. "I used to be scared of things—a monster hiding in my closet or under my bed—but I outgrew it."

"David's right," Calvin said. "I need to get over it."

"Come on, we're wasting time. Let's check out the sideshow attractions." David led the group past several food wagons: hotdogs and hamburgers, popcorn, funnel cakes, cotton candy, and more.

"Look. They have a carousel this year." Rebecca was eager to ride.

"Seriously?" David scowled, but gave in and followed his friends onto the ride.

Calvin climbed atop one of the wooden horses next to Rebecca and tried to push the image of the cowboy clown from his mind.

"Yee-haw," David poked fun at the ride as the carousel started revolving in accompaniment of a whimsical tune.

Calvin laughed and glanced back at him, but his breath suddenly caught in his throat when his gaze fell on an unexpected sight that chilled his bones. The wide-mouthed cowboy clown was on the ride with them, and just as before, he pointed at his eye and mouthed the words: I've got my eye on you.

Calvin squeezed his eyes shut. "Go away," he whispered under his breath. "Go. Away."

Rebecca leaned toward him. "What's wrong?"

"The cowboy clown, he's on the carousel, behind us." Calvin pointed but did not turn around.

"Are you sure?" Rebecca turned and looked. "I don't see him."

Calvin mustered the courage to glace back. "He's gone."

The horse that had carried the wide-mouthed clown was now without a rider.

"I swear, he was there. He must have jumped off the carousel." Calvin needed Rebecca to believe him, but when she drew in her bottom lip and her brow furrowed in concern, he decided to say nothing more.

Exiting the carousel, David made it known that he'd overheard Calvin and Rebecca's conversation. "You were the only clown on that ride. So, you think the clown's out to get you? Maybe it's a clown conspiracy," he taunted. "You're bonkers, Calvin."

"Shut up, David," Rebecca jumped to Calvin's defense. "You're being mean." She narrowed her eyes at him.

"Come on, guys, don't fight," Trina told her friends. "Enough about the clown. We're here to have some fun. Look." She pointed. "I see the freak show banner."

They navigated toward the banner.

COME ONE, COME ALL,
AND SEE THE
FIENDISH FREAKS OF ARAH!

They stopped to read additional banners that showcased the exhibited attractions awaiting them inside.

- ALUNECA THE SNAKEWOMAN.
- A CREATURE FROM YOUR WORST NIGHTMARES, SOPARLA THE GATORMAN.
- DINCOLO DE CERUL. YES, HE CAME FROM BEYOND THE SKY. COME SEE THE BIG-EYED ALIEN.
- TREIORI THE THREE-EYED, FORK-TONGUED GIRL FROM THE NETHERWORLD.

AND MANY OTHER FREAKISH WONDERS.

Entering the midst of the oddities, Calvin abruptly stopped when he caught sight of the cowboy clown standing near the Soparla the Gatorman attraction. The wide-mouthed fiend was once again pointing to his eye and mouthing the words: I've got my eye on you.

This eerily familiar clown, with his grotesque mouth that appeared to grow wider each time he appeared, was Calvin's greatest fear, a disconcerting sight that filled him with utter fright.

"Calvin?" Rebecca turned to see why he had stopped. "Do you want to see the Gatorman?"

Calvin started to point out the clown's position, but in the split second he had looked away, the clown had vanished.

"Yeah." David aimed for the Soparla entrance. "A half-gator, half-man creature from your worst nightmares. I've got to see this."

Calvin kept a watchful eye out for the cowboy clown as they entered the attraction. He was certain that the stalker was trailing his every move, he just didn't know why.

"Why me?" he mumbled under his breath. "Why do you terrorize *me*?"

Calvin had encountered this nightmarish clown every year while visiting The Astonishing Circus of Arah! and in each instance the wide-mouthed terror pointed at his eye and said: I've got my eye on you.

"There he is. Soparla the Gatorman." Rebecca clung to Calvin's arm.

Standing in a dark, curtained room, a strange, gator-like creature hissed at them from behind a thick wall of glass. He was fearsomely large, and his face was marbled with human-like flesh, a hauntingly horrific sight that caused the girls to scream.

"It's just a mutant alligator." David laughed.

Calvin wasn't so sure. He saw the features of a man within that reptilian creature's face and feared that there was more to The Astonishing Circus of Arah! than most people realized. Something truly fiendish.

Over the next hour, Calvin, David, Rebecca, and

Trina went through several more freak show attractions, finding each as horrific as the first.

"It's just about time for the show." David tapped his watch. "We should head inside the big top and find some seats."

En route to the main event, they came upon one last attraction called the Montage of Mirrors.

"There are so many new things to see this year," Trina said. "Let's go in. It won't take long."

Calvin followed his friends through the entrance and into a narrow corridor lined with antique mirrors of various shapes and sizes. Stepping in front of a tall mirror, he pressed a button marked "push" and an animated background scene filled the frame—a cemetery astir with restless spirits and eerily glowing under the light of a full moon.

"This is so cool. Our images are projected into moving scenes." David was impressed with the special effects. "Look, I'm being chased by zombies. It's a zombie apocalypse." He pretended to run, and his image within the animated scene matched his movements. "How do they do this?"

"Technology," Trina answered.

"Or mirror trickery," Rebecca said. "Hence, the Montage of Mirrors."

"These are unreal." David moved from mirror to

mirror, eventually disappearing around a corner.

Trina and Rebecca followed, but Calvin lagged behind when he spotted the cowboy clown in one of the animated scenes, shuddering at the sight of him, yet again, pointing at his eye and mouthing those six chilling words: I've got my eye on you.

Calvin whirled around expecting to find the wide-mouthed clown standing behind him, but he was alone in the corridor. He then stumbled back with a start when every mirror in the corridor simultaneously activated and the dreadful clown suddenly appeared in each animated scene, taunting Calvin with the only words he'd ever spoken to him: I've got my eye on you.

"Why are you doing this?" Calvin's heart rate sped as he made a 360° turn in search of his tormenter. "Stop following me. Leave me alone."

He raced to the end of the corridor and followed a short maze to an adjoining room where he caught up with his friends.

"There you are." Rebecca rushed toward him. "What happened?"

"I-I just wanted to see all of the scenes," Calvin told her, mentioning nothing about the clown.

He was in no mood for any more of David's ridicule; however, after what he'd just experienced, he was beginning to wonder if his friend might be right about his sanity after all. Maybe he was going bonkers.

"Let's go. I don't want to miss any of the show." David hurried the group toward the big top and headed inside, claiming four seats in the upper bleachers.

Calvin, still rattled by the happening in the Montage of Mirrors, nearly jumped out of his seat when a cannon blast announced the start of the extravaganza. The ringmaster then appeared amid a blaring band of brass horns and percussion, welcoming the audience to The Astonishing Circus of Arah!

Calvin tried to forget about the wide-mouthed cowboy clown and focus on the show that quickly transitioned from act to act. Among the performers were fire jugglers with burning torches, big cat animal tamers, death defying stuntmen, flying trapeze acts, tightrope walkers, acrobatics, and of course...clowns.

"They are hilarious." David laughed at the clowns' comedic performance that showcased a tiny white horse that spoofed the previous act of trick riding on full-size horses.

The big top roared with laughter.

"Look." Rebecca leaned toward Calvin. "It's that cowboy clown." She pointed. "He's looking right at us."

Calvin squirmed in his seat when the wide-mouthed clown started climbing the bleachers in their direction. "What is he doing?" His heart pounded.

The sinister character held his hat in one hand, allowing full view of his ragdoll hair that moved in an unnatural, unearthly fashion as he grew close and closer to Calvin and his friends.

"You're right, Calvin. He really is kind of creepy," David whispered.

The cowboy clown stopped at the end of their aisle and pointed at his eye. "I've got my eye on you."

With a fixed stare on Calvin, he slowly redirected his finger at him, crooking it three times.

"I think he wants you to be part of the act," Trina said. "What are you going to do?"

Calvin shuddered, his blood turning cold in his veins as he stared into the nightmarish clown's painted face, thinking that the makeup looked too perfect...too real.

"Rebecca reached for his arm. "You don't have to do this, Calvin."

"I'm not." He jumped to his feet. "I'm getting out of here. I'll wait for you outside, by the popcorn vendor." He turned and quickly exited the opposite side of the bleachers.

Outside the tent, he found a quiet spot to catch his breath and calm down, only to be struck with absolute terror seconds later when a menacing voice drift from the darkness, uttering six menacing words that sent shivers down his spine: "I've got my eye on you."

Calvin spun around and stood face-to-face with the wide-mouthed clown. "Why are you always following me? What do you want from me?"

"It's time for you to join the act, Calvin Cullen." The clown's wide mouth stretched from ear to ear.

This was the first time the clown had communicated more than those six unnerving words: I've got my eye on you.

"I've been waiting a long time for this day to come." The clown drew closer. "We share the mark." He pulled off a leather glove, revealing a dime-sized birthmark on his left palm. "I am George Cullen, your uncle."

"You are George, my dad's brother?" Calvin remembered seeing a picture of him in a family album, now understanding why he'd always seemed so eerily familiar. "Dad said you disappeared from a circus when you were eighteen."

"Yes." The wide-mouthed cowboy clown nodded. "This very circus. The Astonishing Circus of Arah!"

"So, you ran away with the circus, to what, become a clown?" Calvin tried to make sense of what he was conveying.

"Not exactly." George never took his eyes off Calvin. "The circus claimed me because of the Cullen curse."

"The Cullen curse? What do you mean?" Calvin had never heard of a family curse.

"In the early eighteen hundreds, our ancestor Lorcán Alastar Cullen, stole a priceless artifact from a circus owner—a demon named Arah. As punishment for his thievery, Lorcán was branded with a mark on his thieving hand, and his bloodline was cursed. From that day forth, any descendent born with that birthmark in their palm would be cursed to continue paying for Lorcán's crime by serving in Arah's circus, known then, and now, as The Astonishing Circus of Arah!"

Calvin looked at his own marked hand in horror. "I bear that mark."

"Yes. It's your turn," George told him.

"You expect me to take your place?" Calvin could hardly believe what he was hearing.

"A current prisoner can only be freed if a marked Cullen takes his place," George explained. "You will become immortal. You will not age while in the service of Arah. I could have remained eighteen forever, but the thirty years I've spent as a clown feels like an eternity. I waited a long time for a blood descendent bearing the mark to come along, and when you finally appeared, I kept an eye on you, patiently waiting until your eighteenth birthday. That was Lorcán Alastar Cullen's age when he stole from Arah, and the age you had to be to take my place, a time that has finally come."

Without warning, George grabbed Calvin's left hand, and when their birthmarks touched, a rush of energy encompassed them.

"What's happening?" Calvin felt strange and doubled over, aware of being enveloped in a red, swirling mist.

"Don't worry. Someday, another descendent will bear the mark," George told him, "then, you will do the same to them that I have done to you. It is the curse of being a marked Cullen."

When the mist cleared, Calvin looked up at George, but he was no longer a clown. He was now a normal-looking eighteen-year-old boy.

"You look just like the picture I saw of you in the family album. You haven't aged." Calvin gaped at him in puzzlement.

"Nor will you, nephew." George turned and calmly walked away. "You are now in the service of Arah." His words trailed behind him.

Calvin, having no strength to chase after him, heard his friends calling out his name and staggered toward them.

"He's around here somewhere." Rebecca's voice held concern. "He said he would wait by the popcorn vendor," she told David and Trina.

"Did you see that guy we just passed, he was wearing the same hat and clothes that the cowboy clown was wearing," Trina noticed. "That's so weird."

Calvin could hear his friends talking and knew they had just seen George.

"Something doesn't feel right. Where is he?" Rebecca called out for Calvin again, gasping in shock and turning as white as a ghost when her gaze fell on a familiar wide-mouthed clown stumbling toward them, his black ragdoll hair moving in an unnatural manner, just as it had with the cowboy clown. "That-that clown," she stammered, "he's wearing Cal-Calvin's clothes. HE'S WEARING CALVIN'S CLOTHES!"

Rebecca's scream stopped Calvin dead in his tracks, and when he caught sight of his reflection in a pane of glass, he released his own anguished cry at the horrid sight of his painted face, ball nose, and wide, grotesque mouth.

"Where is Calvin?" David yelled out. "What have you done with our friend?"

Calvin took one last look at Rebecca, Trina, and David before fleeing into the night, knowing his life would never be the same. From this time forth, he would spend his days paying for his ancestor's crime by performing in The Astonishing Circus of Arah! This was his sad fate, but he was not without hope, for he knew that one day he would find the next marked Cullen and pass the curse on to that unfortunate relative. Yes, someday another descendent of Lorcán Alastar Cullen would bear the mark, giving Calvin the opportunity to do the same wretched thing to that relation that George had done to him. It was just a matter of time. He just had to wait.

"And when I find you, I will keep a close eye on you until your eighteenth birthday." Calvin pointed at his eye. "A very close eye on you."

Vanderstein Castle.

"Clowns. They give me the shivers. And that's no easy feat. Like the story says, the thought of not being able to see the true identity of a person hiding beneath a colorful costume and makeup is just creepy."

Bam, bam, bam!

"What do you suppose is going on down there in the basement? Yes, it does sound like a war zone. And the clawing inside the walls is worse than ever. But I wouldn't worry. I assume Roger has the matter well in hand. He is, after all, an expert in his field. So, for the moment, let's do our best to ignore the troublesome sounds and move on to one more story. This one is titled 'Classroom 202.'"

CLASSROOM 202

Every kid in town knew that the second floor of the old two-story school was haunted. We all knew the story of the fire that had destroyed the upper level of the building forty years earlier, killing Bemmon Miller, a science teacher who taught in classroom 202. There was even a rhyme that had been passed down since the time of the fire:

> Stay out of classroom 202
> Or Mr. Miller will get you.
> If you step beyond the door,
> You'll disappear forevermore.

It was Friday, October 13, the anniversary of the fire, and a lot of kids were talking about the old urban legend. Melanie, who sat in the lunchroom with her friends, did not believe in ghosts, and she certainly did not believe that the second floor of the old school building was haunted.

"I wonder why they never rebuilt the second floor?" Lori poked at her unappealing lunch. "They use the first floor for the school office, but the second floor has been sealed off for forty years. Don't you find that strange?"

"My dad told me about Mr. Miller, remembering him from his old school days, when he attended school here forty years ago. He said Mr. Miller had wild black hair and always wore a white lab coat. Everyone said he was a genius scientist, and he was rumored to have been working on some bizarre experiment before the fire." James shared what he knew. "Something to do with creating matter."

"Yeah. I heard that too." Their friend, Brad, sat down at the table. "The principle fired him when he found out he was performing dangerous experiments here, at school."

"I guess Mr. Miller was getting revenge when he burnt the school down," James concluded. "And he died in the process."

"But his body was never found." Brad's brow arched high as he widened his eyes. "Spooky, if you ask me."

"I don't believe any of it," Melanie scoffed.

"So, you'd go up there? You'd look in classroom 202?" Brad put her on the spot. "If I dared you?"

"No," Lori protested. "Don't do it. Over the years, any kid who ever dared to go up there was never seen again. That's why it's sealed off. Like the rhyme says:

Stay out of classroom 202
Or Mr. Miller will get you.
If you step beyond the door,
You'll disappear forevermore."

"I told you, Lori, I don't believe any of it." Melanie refused to be swayed from her fixed opinion. "It's just an urban legend."

"My dad said that the only person to ever go up there and actually return is now in a psych ward. After opening the door to classroom 202, he went crazy, and now continually repeats the rhyme. They say he just mumbles it over and over again," James told them.

"Sorry, guys. Like I said, I just don't believe any of it." Melanie stood up with her food tray in hand. "I'd accept your dare, Brad, if there was a way to get up to the second floor. But it's locked up tight."

"I can get the key." Brad's lips stretched into a cunning grin. "The only person in the office right now is Mrs. Beechley and getting around her is a piece of cake."

"Okay," Melanie said. "If you get the key, you've got a dare."

"Meet me in front of the old building in ten minutes." Brad gathered his things and darted away.

Ten minutes later, Melanie, James, and Lori found Brad waiting for them by the entrance of the supposedly haunted schoolhouse.

"I told you getting the key would be a piece of cake." He proudly dangled the key in front of him before handing it to Melanie. "But how will I know if you actually open the door to classroom 202?"

"I'll go with you, Melanie," James offered. "I'll be your witness."

"Are you sure?" Melanie didn't want to get him into trouble.

"I want to," he assured her. "I want to see what's up there." He pushed open the door leading into the building. "Let's go."

"Be careful sneaking past the office," Brad warned his friends. "Mrs. Beechley was sitting at the front counter a few minutes ago."

Melanie nodded, and she and James slipped,

unseen, past the downstairs office and stealthily maneuvered around a roped-off staircase. Easing up the stairs, to the second floor, they came to a locked door at the top of the landing.

"I sure hope this is the right key." Melanie placed it in the lock and turned it, hearing a click.

Without warning, the door swung open, and an icy burst of air struck them with biting force.

"What was that?" James hesitated to step beyond the door. "This is creepy."

"You can't chicken out on me." Melanie grabbed his hand and pulled him through the doorway and into an upstairs hallway. "You're my witness. You have to see me open the door."

Forging ahead, Melanie pulled James past the first door marked classroom 200, releasing his hand as they eased along the cold, stuffy hallway.

"Classroom 201," she whispered as she passed the second door. "The next door should be 202."

"I can't believe I volunteered for this." James, who had yet to pass classroom 201, had slowed to a halt.

"This is it." Melanie stopped at the third door—classroom 202."

"This is as far as I go." James clung to the wall. "I'm not getting any closer."

Melanie reached for the doorknob and slowly

turned it, pausing mid-turn when she heard a faint, ghostly voice say:

Stay out of classroom 202
Or Mr. Miller will get you.
If you step beyond the door,
You'll disappear forevermore.

Melanie looked at James. "Did you hear that?"

James nodded; his eyes wide with fright. "This floor really is haunted. Please, Melanie, don't open that door."

"There has to be a logical explanation," she told him. "I bet Brad is up here, right now, trying to scare us. He's probably getting a good laugh at our expense. I bet he came up the fire escape." She continued to turn the doorknob. "But it's not going to work, Brad, because I don't believe in ghosts."

With those five words, she thrust the door open and stepped into classroom 202.

"Melanie, what do you see?" James called out, but she did not respond. "Melanie?" He mustered all his courage, rushed to the door, and peered inside. "Nooo!" He gripped the edge of the doorjamb to keep from being pulled into a spiraling vortex.

Classroom 202 was a doorway to another realm of

existence, and within the spiraling mass of energy, James saw Melanie being dragged to a desk by a man with wild black hair and wearing a white lab coat. It was Mr. Miller, and he had Melanie.

"Melanie!" James cried out, drawing the attention of several hollow-eyed kids trapped along with Melanie in the classroom beyond the vortex.

Petrified, his body fell numb when the ghostly kids, all staring directly at him, began chanting the classroom 202 rhyme:

Stay out of classroom 202
Or Mr. Miller will get you.
If you step beyond the door,
You'll disappear forevermore.

As the vortex started to close, the last thing James saw before letting go of the doorjamb and running for his life, was a final glimpse of Melanie. He would never forget her hollow eyes and dead stare—a sight that would haunt him for the rest of his life.

***

Downstairs, Lori and Brad intercepted James as he fled the building, eager for an update. But when they questioned him about Melanie and the haunted second floor, all he could say was:

> Stay out of classroom 202
> Or Mr. Miller will get you.
> If you step beyond the door,
> You'll disappear forevermore.

Vanderstein Castle.

"Melanie really should have listened to Lori and stayed out of room 202. Now, she has disappeared forever, and James, who was utterly traumatized, will never be the same."

Bam, bam, bam! Bang, bang, bang!

"I sure hope Roger has more than a hammer down there, because it sounds like he's having some major difficulties. Pest control and extermination can be a hazardous line of work if one is not properly equipped for the task. I probably should have made sure he had the appropriate qualifications to manage any type of infestation, but his business card does specifically state:

For infestations big or small,

Roger Felis kills them all.

Yes, I know it doesn't sound good, but still, I'd like

to give him the benefit of the doubt. If things have not improved by the time we finish this next story, I'll certainly check on him. Now, let's continue. This one is called 'A Bad, Bad Thing.'"

A BAD, BAD THING

At the witching hour, a mysterious figure emerged from a distant darkness. Draped in a sable cape, the entity moved in accompaniment of three feral cats, a sight that rattled my cold bones and filled me with paralyzing terror.

Yowls emanating from the animals sent me stumbling backward, upon which I attempted to cry out, but no sound would part my restricted throat.

"Jyna, you've gone and done it again." The individual's cape blew wildly behind him. "This is a bad, bad thing."

I said nothing and tried to run, but my legs were

stiff and uncooperative, causing me to trip over a raised slab of stone and fall facedown on the ground. Feeling no pain, I managed to roll over, and by the light of the moon, I saw that I was lying atop a grave. I then glimpsed the epitaph on the headstone and shuddered when I saw the name. I was in the cemetery, and this was my grandfather's grave.

I scrambled behind the headstone and watched the caped figure drift amid the graves. I had no memory of going to the cemetery, wondering how, and why, I was there.

"It'll take a little time for your body to loosen up. It's the rigor mortis," the stranger spoke in a calm voice. "My name is Benjamin. I'm afraid my pet is responsible for what has happened. You see, she accidentally jumped over your grave."

I didn't understand. Rigor mortis? My grave? Was is possible that I was...dead?

"You had just been buried, three days ago, when Jyna went and did this bad, bad thing." The stranger bent down and picked up one of the lanky cats.

I had no idea what the caped man, Benjamin, was talking about, concluding that Jyna was the cat. But what exactly had Jyna done?

"You're a bad, bad kitty, Jyna. A bad, bad Kitty who's done a bad, bad thing." He stroked the cat. "But it wasn't on purpose. This time, it *was* an accident."

Benjamin looked directly at me, and I glimpsed his pale, thin face.

"Chasing her prey, she did not see the new grave— your grave." He put the cat down.

I struggled to speak, managing to utter a slurred, "W-what?"

"You don't yet understand." Benjamin moved closer. "Look at your attire. You are wearing burial clothes."

I realized that I was dressed in my best Sunday suit, albeit, torn and soiled.

"Look at your hands, used to claw your way out of the grave," he then said.

I looked and saw that my fingernails were not only unusually long, but also ripped and embedded with dirt.

"Now, look at your burial plot." He pointed to an unearthed grave.

I looked and knew that it was, indeed, my grave.

"Jyna did a bad thing the night you were buried, but she came and told me, and now, three nights later, I'm here to help you."

Observing the three cats, I noticed the odd way they moved through the cemetery, never crossing directly over a grave.

"What J-Jyna, w-what?" I wanted to know what

Jyna had done to me.

"Don't worry. Your speech will improve. You've been three days in the ground. Just give it time. That's something you now have plenty of—time."

"W-what J-Jyna do?" I needed an explanation.

"I told you. She accidentally jumped over your grave."

I didn't understand what the cat had to do with my predicament. "W-what?"

Benjamin now stood within arm's reach in front of me.

"You see, when a cat jumps over a corpse, even shortly after burial, the deceased becomes the undead." He placed a hand on my shoulder, and I observed his long, talon-like fingernails. "You, my friend, are the undead—a vampire—fangs and all."

Looking down at Jyna who dropped a dead rat at my feet, I knew she was sorry for jumping over my grave, but the stranger was right, this was a bad thing. A bad, bad thing. For I was suddenly gripped by an insatiable hunger, and this small rat was nothing more than an appetizer.

***

Three years earlier

In the mid of night, Benjamin Vanderstein sat next to an unearthed grave, wondering how he had gotten there. Furthering his confusion, Jyna—his cat—laid against him, happily purring.

"W-what?" He tried to speak, but his words would not come.

Why can't I speak? He didn't understand. *Fangs.* He felt them in his mouth. *"Why do I have fangs?"*

He looked at his clothes. He wore a soiled suit. He looked at his hands. His nails were long and curved, ripped, and impacted with earth. He tried to stand, but his legs were stiff and uncooperative.

I must have died, he thought. *I must have been buried and then crawled out of my grave.*

At that moment, Jyna suddenly ran off and vanished in the distant darkness, leaving Benjamin alone in the cemetery. Helpless and abandoned, he surrendered to his limited range of motion and collapsed next to his grave. He hadn't lain there long when he heard the rustling of an approaching animal.

"Jyna. There you are." He sat up when he caught

sight of her emerging from the darkness, bearing a gift—a large rat.

Without thought, he snatched up the rat and devoured it, horrified by his lack of self-control and realizing, in that instant, the monster he had become.

"Jyna, what have you done to me?" Benjamin knew what she had done. "This is a bad thing. A bad, bad thing."

She meowed and affectionately rubbed against him.

"I always had a feeling that you understood everything I said. I never should have mentioned that when a cat jumps over a corpse that the deceased comes back as the undead." He stood up and brushed dirt off his suit. "I guess you missed me, huh?" He looked down at the cat. "With that being the case, I could never be angry with you. We'll just have to make the best of a bad thing." He bent down and picked her up. "Thank you for the rat, but I'll have to find something more...satisfying. I've never been so hungry. So very, very hungry."

Jyna meowed.

"Yes. It will be morning soon. We should head home." He somehow understood what she said. "Now that I'm a vampire, I'll need to be somewhere nice and dark by sunrise."

Jyna meowed again.

"No. You're not a bad cat. You're a good cat, Jyna. But you must never jump over a corpse again. Raising the dead is a bad thing. A bad, bad thing."

Vanderstein Castle.

"Poor little Jyna. She didn't mean to do anything wrong. But sometimes good kitties do bad, bad things."

Bam, bam, bam! Bang, bang, bang! Nooo! Ahhh!

"Speaking of a bad, bad thing, that doesn't sound good at all. I think I should hurry on down to the basement and check on our professional exterminator, Roger."

The host entrusts the book he's been reading to one of his guests, his long, talon-like fingernails grating against the leather cover as he pulls his hand away.

"Read this final poem while I step away."

He taps a page with his bony finger.

"This one titled 'The Coffin Where Sean Sleeps.'"

THE COFFIN
WHERE SEAN SLEEPS

This is the coffin where Sean sleeps.

This is the grave
That holds the coffin where Sean sleeps.

This is the headstone,
That marks the grave
That holds the coffin where Sean sleeps.

This is the oak,

That shades the headstone,
That marks the grave
That holds the coffin where Sean sleeps.

This is the wind,
That blows the old oak,
That shades the headstone,
That marks the grave
That holds the coffin where Sean sleeps.

This is the cemetery,
With the whispering winds,
And the old mossy oak,
That shades the headstone,
That marks the grave
That holds the coffin where Sean sleeps.

This is the road,
That leads to the cemetery,
With the whispering winds,
And the old mossy oak,
That shades the headstone,
That marks the grave
That holds the coffin where Sean sleeps.

This is the hearse,

That travels the road,
That leads to the cemetery,
With the whispering winds,
And the old mossy oak,
That shades the headstone,
That marks the grave
That holds the coffin where Sean sleeps.

This is the undertaker,
Who drives the hearse,
That travels the road,
That leads to the cemetery,
With the whispering winds,
And the old mossy oak,
That shades the headstone,
That marks the grave
That holds the coffin where Sean sleeps.

This is the hymn,
That the undertaker sings,
Who drives the hearse,
While traveling the road,
That leads to the cemetery,
With the whispering winds,
And the old mossy oak,
That shades the headstone,

That marks the grave
That holds the coffin where Sean sleeps.

This is the spirit that hitched a ride,
After hearing the hymn,
That the undertaker sang,
Who drove the hearse,
While traveling the road,
That led to the cemetery,
With the whispering winds,
And the old mossy oak,
That shades the headstone,
That marks the grave
That holds the coffin where Sean slept.

Vanderstein Castle.

"I hope I wasn't away too long. I'm afraid I couldn't find Roger. It seems he has simply...vanished. He apparently wasn't the expert exterminator he claimed to be."

The host takes his book back from the guest he'd entrusted it to.

"What? A cat followed me in? Well, that's no surprise. I actually have three cats."

The guests scream and jump onto their chairs.

"What's wrong? The cat has what? A mutated rodent? Oh, Jyna, what have you brought me?"

The host reaches down and accepts the gift from his cat.

"Jyna is a good cat. A very good cat. She has, however, done one or two bad things over the years, but sometimes you just have to make the best of a bad thing.

Like I told my friend—the author who wrote this book—I could never be angry with her."

The five guests scream again and race for the door when several mutated rodents gnaw through the wall of the library and scurry into the room. The host runs after his guests, watching from the front door as they flee the castle amid an unrelenting storm.

"Well, Jyna, it looks like we'll have to handle this infestation ourselves."

The host allows his long, sharp fangs to emerge and bites into the rodent Jyna brought him.

"It was nice having company tonight, but I believe this is the last we'll see of them."

Jyna meows.

"No. They won't be back. But at least they stayed long enough to finish the collection of scary stories that did indeed give them...a fright in the night."

SCARY STORIES

FOR

A FRIGHT IN THE NIGHT